Science Makes It Work
The Wonder of Color

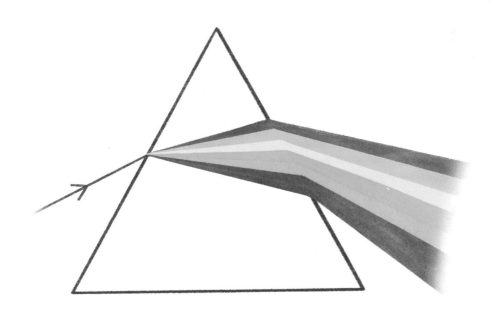

Catherine Stier

illustrated by
Floss Pottage

Albert Whitman & Company
Chicago, Illinois

James's school buzzed with news of the art contest.
 "The winner gets to paint their own design right on the school library wall," James told his dad that evening. "For *everyone* to see."

But when James glanced at the drawings taped up in his bedroom, he sighed.

"How can I enter the contest? I don't have an idea that's big or important or colorful enough."

"Maybe we can find some art to inspire you this weekend," Dad suggested.

That Saturday, James saw a playground covered in cheery chalk drawings...

a bakery decorated with a sweet mural...

and a zooming city bus decked out in a lively design.

At the city's art museum, James stopped in front of a very large, very old painting. The colors glowed—cool blues, burning reds, sunny yellows.

"Pretty amazing," said Dad.

"Yeah, but now I have questions," James said. "How does paint get its color? And how do artists find just the right shades?"

"Why not ask the expert over there?" Dad suggested.

"Paint is made by adding a source of color, called a pigment, to other chemicals, including a substance called a binder, which holds everything together," the museum guide explained. "Many of today's pigments were developed in labs. But throughout history, people have made colorful paints from berries, dirt, gems, and even insects."

"Wow," said James, gazing at the paintings with new wonder. "And artists can create endless shades by mixing different paint colors together," the guide added.

Back in his neighborhood,
James noticed colors everywhere—
in the bright sky...

among his neighbors' flowers...

and in his sister Kara's drawings.

I still have lots of questions about colors, James thought, *like where does color come from? How do our eyes see it?*

"All light is made up of waves," James read to Dad from an article online. "While white light, like sunlight or a flashlight beam, appears colorless, it is actually made up of light waves in all the colors of the rainbow."

James continued reading, "When light hits an object, some light waves get absorbed by the object and others get reflected, or bounced, away. Our eyes see the color of the wave that is reflected off the object."

"So a red ball absorbs all the color waves...*except* red, right?" said Dad.

"Right," said James. "We're seeing the color that is not part of the ball."

"Pretty cool stuff," Dad said.

"Yeah, but it's still hard to imagine how white light is full of colors," said James. "Can we try an experiment? This article shows how to make a homemade version of a prism."

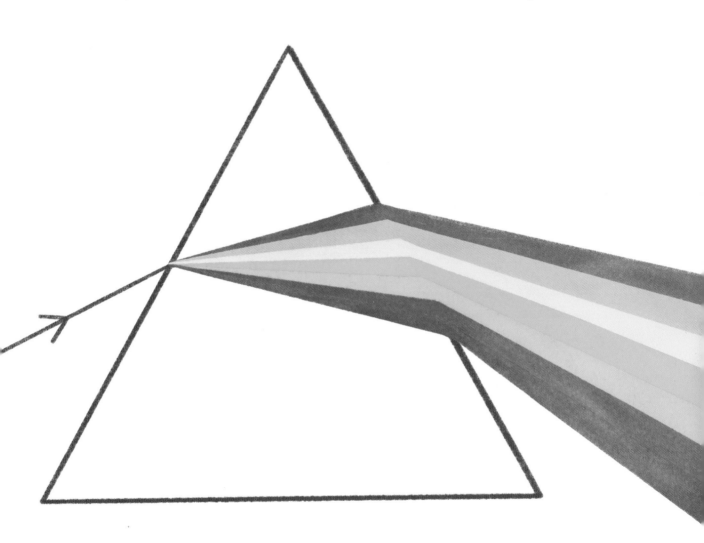

"What's a prism?" Kara chimed in.

"It's something that can bend, or refract, light to show the color waves separately," James explained. "Dad, if you'll get a glass of water, I can do the rest."

While Dad filled a glass, James grabbed a flashlight and placed large sheets of white paper on the floor. As Dad steadied the glass on the table's edge, James angled the flashlight toward the water.

"If this works, the water in the glass will refract the light waves," James explained, "and we should see..."
James clicked on the flashlight.

"A rainbow!" Kara exclaimed.
"Yep. Red, orange, yellow,
green, blue, indigo, and violet,"
James said.

In art class on Monday, James saw Lily and Diego working on their contest entries. Both were drawing scenes from their favorite books. "Those look great," he told them.

"Are you entering the contest?" Diego asked.

"I want to, but I haven't started yet," James admitted. "I'm still trying to figure out my design."

"You can borrow an art book, if that would help," his art teacher, Ms. Vega, offered.

As James flipped through the book at home that afternoon, Kara pointed to a page.

"What's that?" she asked.

"Hmm. That's the color wheel," James said. "It shows that red, yellow, and blue are primary colors. They can be mixed together to make what are called secondary colors, like green, orange, and violet."

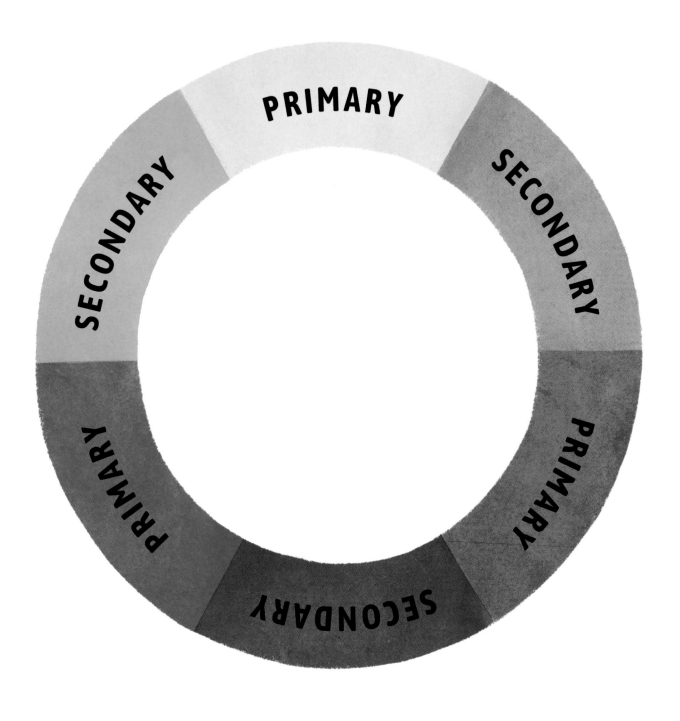

Then he peered closer. "See how green is here between blue and yellow? That means mixing blue and yellow paint should make green."

"Let's try it!" said Kara.

With Kara's paint set, they experimented.

"Maybe mixing all three primary colors will make the brightest color of all!" Kara said.

"Nope." James laughed at the brown puddle on the paper.
"But I might need this color too!"

He and Kara kept mixing new colors, adding a few brushstrokes of each to small paper scraps. They rearranged the scraps into their favorite color combinations.

"Now can we paint a picture together?" Kara asked.

"Sure," James said, setting the scraps aside. *I'll work on my contest design later,* he thought.

But that night, James tossed and turned. The contest entry was due soon, and he didn't even have an idea yet! Besides, Lily and Diego's drawings were so good—how would the teachers ever choose just one winner?

Then James remembered the fun he had creating art with Kara and how her stars and rocket added something special to his space scene.

Suddenly James had an idea...a big, colorful, amazing idea.

He worked excitedly on his entry all the next day.

On Friday everyone hushed as Ms. Vega announced
the contest winner:

"Although only one student's entry was chosen, we truly have many winners," she said. "We've selected James's design of a giant open book, and it comes with a special treat: James invites everyone at Shady Oaks School to collaborate and paint a scene from their favorite story on the book's pages!"

James's classmates looked surprised. Then they celebrated.

And soon the big, important, and *very* colorful art the students created together brightened the library walls for all to see.

To Karen, a great friend and a gifted
educator who brings a special kind of light
and color to this world!—CS

Thank you to James for all your love and
support, and for cheering me on—FP

Library of Congress Cataloging-in-Publication data
is on file with the publisher.
Text copyright © 2022 by Catherine Stier
Illustrations copyright © 2022 by Albert Whitman & Company
Illustrations by Floss Pottage
First published in the United States of America in 2022
by Albert Whitman & Company
ISBN 978-0-8075-7268-9 (hardcover)
ISBN 978-0-8075-7269-6 (ebook)
Printed in China
10 9 8 7 6 5 4 3 2 1 WKT 26 25 24 23 22 21

Design by Rick DeMonico

For more information about Albert Whitman & Company,
visit our website at www.albertwhitman.com.